COUNTDOWN
TO
Christmas

written and illustrated by BILL PEET

GOLDEN GATE JUNIOR BOOKS
San Carlos • California

To my grandson
TIMOTHY
who is a firm believer
in Santa Claus

Copyright © 1972 by William B. Peet
All rights reserved
ISBNs: Trade 0-87464-198-5 Library 0-87464-199-3
Library of Congress catalog card number 72-78394
Lithographed in the United States of America

’Twas countdown to Christmas, the fourteenth of December,
Way back in the sixties—’twas the jet age, remember?
And the Jolly Old Santa Toy Corporation,
An old-fashioned factory with no automation,
Was going full blast, full tilt, and full swing,
With the toy-making elves all doing their thing.
They’d be done before Christmas, they had never failed yet.
Just the same, Santa worried, he was in a big sweat.

"We've got to get with it," the old fellow would say
As he made the rounds of the factory each day.
"We don't dare miss a thing in the way of new toys
For this new generation of mod girls and boys."
This angered old Ezra, the boss of the elves,
Who okayed the toys that were stacked on the shelves.

"Dad-blast-it!" he snapped, "I keep checking the list—
For all I can see not one item's been missed.
We've got all the latest in scale-model trains,
We've got jets and copters and new-fangled planes;
Dune buggies, dragsters, all kinds of haulers,
Earthmovers, dozers, tractors and crawlers."
"Cool it," cried Santa, "like that's enough!
Tomorrow we'd better start loading the stuff."

And he hauled his old leather sack off the hook,
Held it up to the light, then after one look,
Santa exclaimed, "What a beat up old rag!
What a sad sack, it's all shot, it's a drag!"
"That sack," grumbled Ezra, "has served many a season.
We've held onto the thing for a mighty good reason."
"Good reason or not," Santa gruffly replied,
"What I do with the sack is for me to decide.

"It's a worthless old relic, one total loss."
And he opened the window and gave it a toss.
The wind caught the sack, it took off like a kite,
Then in no time at all it had sailed out of sight.

"Now Ezra," said Santa, "don't blow your stack.
I'll get Mrs. Claus to make a new sack."
Then away Santa went to explain to his wife
How he'd tossed out the sack he had used all his life.

"What I need right now is a new one," he said.
"And since you're so sharp with a needle and thread,
Could you dream up a sack that's more like fantastic?
A real far-out satchel of nylon or plastic?"
"I don't like the idea," his wife said with a sigh,
"But then if you insist I can give it a try."

"Real groovy!" cried Santa. "That'll be great!
Now I must bring my old sleigh up to date."
And with cans of spray paint, all colors but red,
He rushed out to the sleigh where it stood in a shed.

Then in a frenzy the frantic old fellow
Cut loose with a blast of synthetic yellow—
A blurp of bright purple, a scriggle of green,
A splotch and a zigzag of ultramarine—

While his eight faithful reindeer gathered about
To stare in amazement, their eyes bugging out.
He kept firing away, to the reindeers' dismay,
Till he'd covered every last inch of the sleigh.

It was one awful mess for all they could see,
And yet Santa seemed just as pleased as could be.
"That's what you call mod," he said with a smile,

"An up-to-date sleigh, at least for awhile.
Next year I'll convert this old sleigh to a jet,
With twin jet engines and a pair of wings yet.

"I'll blast off like a rocket on a radar beam,
Then I won't need to hassle with a reindeer team.
Of course I'll get rid of my Santa Claus suit
And dress like a pilot while I'm going that route.
We're into the jet age—the big thing is speed!
A super jet sleigh is like just what I need."

The reindeer could hardly believe it at first.
Of all the bad news this was by far the worst!
If Santa was really done with the deer
They'd be unemployed by the end of the year.
"We're all washed up," said Dunder, "that's what.
We'll soon be sold on a used reindeer lot."

"Now hold on," said Prancer. "You give up too quick.
It might be that Santa's on what's called a Kick.
There's no need to worry, it's only a phase—
He'll come down to earth in a couple of days."

And Prancer was right—there was no need to worry,
For Santa *did* come down to earth in a hurry.
What brought Santa down was the synthetic sack.
When it was ready and the time came to pack

The elves discovered there was little room in it—
They had filled it with toys in less than a minute.
And when Santa tried to cram in a few more
The toys tumbled out to end up on the floor.

So he finally gave up, he sank down in a chair
With a weary, woebegone sigh of despair.
"The old sack," he muttered, "could hold toys by the ton.
It was never quite full till the very last one."
"I told you," said Ezra, "or I must say I tried.
It was more than a sack, it's what was inside.
There's no way to replace it, that's what's so tragic!
That old sack was special, a thing of pure magic.
A magic that sails your sleigh through the sky
And also helps all your reindeer to fly."

"There's no doubt," said Santa, "that old sack was great.
I've just got to find it before it's too late."
He jerked on a jacket, *ker-plunked* on a cap,
Flung on a wool muffler *ker-whoppity-whap!*
Pulled on some knit mittens and grabbed a flashlight,
Then barged out the door with a hasty "Good night!"

Up there on the snow-swept top of the world
The wind played mean tricks, it swooshed and it swirled.
Which meant the sack could have sailed anywhere—
It might have been tossed ten miles through the air.
So old Santa searched in a roundabout way;
He went on a round and round trip you might say.

First he went south and then circled back west,
Then he decided straight east might be best.
For hours and hours he circled around,
But no sign or a trace of the sack could be found.

He climbed heaps of ice, great frosty white stacks,
To shine his light in the crannies and cracks.
He crawled into a cave, then quickly backed out
When he discovered some bones scattered about.

It just happened to be a polar bear's lair—
How lucky it was the bear wasn't there!
Or he would have finished old Mister Claus
With one quick swipe of his great hairy paws.

"After this I must be more careful," he said,
As he left the cave to go trudging ahead.
By this time his toes were starting to freeze—
He felt the cold creeping up to his knees.
The wind had picked up and now it was snowing.
It was hard to see just where he was going.

And Santa was barely able to stop
One step away from a forty-foot drop.
He took a look down at the foot of the bluff
At the icy-cold sea and that was enough.

"I've had it," groaned Santa, "I've done all I could.
There's no doubt about it, the sack's gone for good."
After making dead sure which direction was right,
Santa headed for home through the freezing-cold night.
Now he was weary, bedraggled and beat.
As he trudged along he was dragging his feet.

He tripped in a ditch, he staggered and stumbled,
Then lost his footing and over he tumbled.

And flat on his whiskers old Santa flopped,
And into a snowdrift his flashlight *ker-plopped!*

What happened next was more like a weird dream.
Just a few yards away in the light's golden beam
He spotted a walrus with a cap on his noggin,
A faded brown baggy beat-up old toboggan.
"Can't blame you for staring," the huge walrus said.
"This cap is ten sizes too big for my head."
"So I'll trade you," said Santa. "Try this cap of mine.
It has a fur lining and should fit you just fine."
"Sounds like a good deal," the big fellow agreed.
"That red cap of yours is a dandy indeed."

When he tried on the cap he found it **too** small,
And he said with a snort, "It won't do at all!"
But by this time old Santa was gone—what I mean,
He had snatched up the sack and deserted the scene.
It was such a great lift to recover the sack
That his feet fairly flew as he galloped on back.

The instant he leaped through the toy factory door,
And plunked down his magical sack on the floor,
Old Ezra's army of hard-working elves
Got busy hauling the toys off the shelves;

Cramming them down in the sack by the ton,
Taking great care not to break even one.
After the packing was well underway
Santa decided to repaint the sleigh.

And even though he was in a great rush,
He painted the sleigh this time with a brush—
With no fancy tricks, to the reindeers' delight—
Just a plain Christmas crimson, lovely and bright.
"That's a billion times better," Santa confessed
As he scurried off to his house to get dressed.

It was getting quite late, it was Christmas Eve,
With just barely time to get ready to leave.
And in half a jiffy the lively old coot
Had **stuffed himself** into his Santa Claus suit.

"They can't call me square," he said with a grin,
"Not while these big bushy beards are still in."
"No one," said his wife, "is more up to date, dear.
You set the style, at least this time of year.

You're far more than a someone who delivers the toys—
You're the spirit of Christmas to most girls and boys."
Then Santa lost his cool, if you please!
He gave Mrs. Claus a big hug and a squeeze.
"And now then," he said, "I've got to split—I mean go."
And he bounced out the door with a merry "Ho Ho!"

The deer greeted Santa with bright smiles on their faces.
They were walking on air as they pranced in their traces.
He was the same old Santa, they liked him that way,

With his old-fashioned sack and his old-fashioned sleigh.
It was just like Christmas—almost but not quite—
But it would be after they'd made their long flight.

And at the crack of the whip and a jolly "Right on!"
They took off like a shot, they were really far-gone.
As they faded from sight Santa called loud and clear,
"A cool Christmas to all! And a groovy New Year!"